KID SQUAD

saves the World

The Snickerblooms and the Age Bug

by John Perritano   Illustrated by Mike Laughead

Calico

An Imprint of Magic Wagon
www.abdopublishing.com

www.abdopublishing.com

Published by Magic Wagon, a division of ABDO, PO Box 398166, Minneapolis, Minnesota 55439. Copyright © 2015 by Abdo Consulting Group, Inc. International copyrights reserved in all countries. No part of this book may be reproduced in any form without written permission from the publisher. Calico™ is a trademark and logo of Magic Wagon.

Printed in the United States of America, North Mankato, Minnesota.
042014
092014

Written by John Perritano
Illustrated by Mike Laughead
Edited by Rochelle Baltzer and Megan M. Gunderson
Cover and interior design by Candice Keimig

Library of Congress Cataloging-in-Publication Data

Perritano, John, author.
  The Snickerblooms and the Age Bug / by John Perritano ;
illustrated by Mike Laughead.
     pages cm. -- (Kid Squad saves the world)
  Summary: When Athena's parents suddenly disappear, she calls on
her friends on the Kid Squad to help figure out what happened--
and uncovers the surprising connection between her parents, a
biological weapon called the Age Bug, and their old enemy Dr.
Alowishus Cobalt.
  ISBN 978-1-62402-041-4
1. Biological weapons--Juvenile fiction. 2. Abduction--Juvenile
fiction. 3. Scientists--Juvenile fiction. 4. Inventions--
Juvenile fiction. 5. Heroes--Juvenile fiction. [1. Biological
weapons--Fiction. 2. Kidnapping--Fiction. 3. Identity--Fiction.
4. Scientists--Fiction. 5. Inventions--Fiction. 6. Heroes--
Fiction.] I. Laughead, Mike, illustrator. II. Title.
  PZ7.P43415Sn 2015
  813.6--dc23
                  2014001052

Table of Contents

Chapter 1

San Francisco: 1987

"Our gooses are cooked if anyone finds out. If anyone suspects what we're up to, you and I will be spending the rest of our lives in prison. You don't want to go to prison, do you Alowishus?"

Dr. Alowishus Cobalt stared out the window of Oxford Grant's office on the 100th floor of the Omni-Tech Tower, which commanded one of the best views of San Francisco. Grant was the powerful owner of Omni-Tech, the world's largest and most important scientific research company.

Cobalt, not yet thirty-five years old, stared blankly out at the city. He saw, but didn't see, the Golden Gate Bridge shimmering in the bright summer sun. A steady breeze whipped the waters of San Francisco Bay into small whitecaps.

Cobalt mumbled.

"I'm sorry, Alowishus, did you say something?" Mr. Grant bellowed, his rather rotund belly bouncing with each syllable.

"I understand, Mr. Grant," Cobalt said softly. "I promise that we'll get the formula and no one will be the wiser. I suspect we will have it in a few more weeks."

"I can't wait that long, Alowishus. You need to get the Snickerblooms' research now and find a way to make it work. Once you get what we want, well, you know what to do, don't you?" Grant asked.

Cobalt remained silent. He stared out the window again and wished that he were somewhere else. He liked Will and Sally Snickerbloom. They were young, they were smart, and they truly wanted to make a difference in the world. They were so nice that they invited him out for pizza every Friday afternoon. No one at Omni-Tech had ever asked Alowishus Cobalt to have lunch, dinner, or even an ice cream cone for that matter. He didn't make friends easily.

It was the summer of 1987, and Will and Sally Snickerbloom—two social activists if ever there were—were using their vast scientific knowledge to help feed the hungry. "If you're not part of the solution, you're part of the problem," Sally liked to say.

It was Sally's idea—the food thing and all. She had this crazy notion that she could modify the genes of a particular strain of wheat so it could grow just about anywhere.

Most people thought the idea was ridiculous. Everyone knew what genes were, but Sally really understood them. Genes determined such things as a person's eye and hair color along with other traits passed from parent to child. Plants had genes, too. Sally hoped to take the best genes and arrange them like flowers in a pot.

Still, manipulating microscopic genes was something out of a science-fiction novel or that TV show *Star Trek* from the '60s. (Will loved to watch the reruns late at night.) Besides, many of Sally's colleagues said it couldn't be done.

Yet, Cobalt understood the implications of Sally's research. He asked the husband-and-wife team to join Omni-Tech. Money was no object. He would find them the best apartment in the city and give them all the support they needed to make their theories reality.

Cobalt brimmed with excitement when he brought the pair to San Francisco. At the time, he too was a young scientist trying to make his mark on the world. If the Snickerblooms were successful, farmers could plant the seeds in the desert, or other dry places, and later harvest bushel upon bushel of wheat. If gene manipulation worked with wheat, it stood to reason that it would work with barley, corn, or any crop for that matter. Millions of people would have tons of food to eat and to sell. They wouldn't be hungry anymore. Their lives would be so much better.

Oxford Grant knew the implications as well. Yet he was intrigued for an entirely different reason. He had hit a brick wall working on a project for a US Army colonel named Tecumseh S. Barnstable. Barnstable wasn't stable at all, and his men, not to mention his superiors, detested him, which was one reason Barnstable wanted to form his own army.

To that end, Barnstable had asked Omni-Tech to develop a biological weapon that would render troops useless on the battlefield. Grant agreed, but it was going to cost a lot of money. No problem, the colonel said. He had access to millions of dollars, all of which he had stolen from the government. Grant nodded and off to work he went, putting his best scientists on the project. Of course, Grant lied and told them they were working on a top-secret army program.

Eventually Grant's scientists came up with a plan to develop a super bacterium, a tiny single-cell organism that would age a person within seconds. Everyone called it the Age Bug. The Age Bug could be placed inside a bomb and exploded over a battlefield. All it took was one whiff, and in moments, a spry, energetic, twenty-year-old soldier would have the frail body of a 100-year-old person now too weak to fight. Grant loved the idea and he pursued its development with vigor.

After months of work, Grant's scientists hit the pause button. As luck would have it, and luck always plays a role in such devious and evil schemes, Cobalt, so young, so idealistic, brought the Snickerblooms' research to Grant's attention.

Everyone agreed that gene manipulation was the missing piece of the Age Bug puzzle. Grant took Cobalt into his confidence and persuaded him to become part of the project. At first, the young genius hesitated to join the sinister plot, but he couldn't turn down Grant's offer of $1 million. Of course, Cobalt had to deceive the Snickerblooms. They could not know the real reason they were hired. It was all hush-hush.

"Let them work out the kinks to this gene manipulation thing," Grant told Cobalt. "Let them figure out the hard parts. Then we can apply their research and finish the Age Bug."

That's how it went for months and months.

Cobalt now remembered how Sally cried when he offered them the job. "Oh, Dr. Cobalt, you won't be sorry," she gushed, tears running down her pale cheeks. "You won't be sorry at all. You, Will, and I are going to help a lot of people."

It seemed so long ago.

¤

"I'm sorry, Alowishus, I didn't hear you," Grant yelled again. His voice jolted Cobalt back to the present. "You know what to do, don't you? You need to get their research, and once you do, well, Sally and Will Snickerbeetle, Snickerdoodle, whatever their name is, must disappear. There's too much money at stake. This needs to happen as quickly as possible."

In the years that followed, reporters often asked Dr. Alowishus Cobalt at what point he turned into a mad and evil scientist. Cobalt never answered, but he knew his fate was decided when he responded to Mr. Oxford Grant on that sunny day in 1987: "Yes, sir. I know what to do. You can count on me."

¤

It was midnight and a blanket of fog had crawled into the city from the bay, shrouding San Francisco in an eerie, misty cocoon. The muffled roar of foghorns from ships moored on the bay sounded ominous, echoing down the dark, dank alleyways near the wharf.

Will and Sally Snickerbloom walked arm in arm toward a rickety old dock, their shadows falling on wet, damp pavement. They held on to each other tight. Sally's high heels clipped noisily on the street. She carried a briefcase packed with their latest research. No one was around.

"Why do you think Dr. Cobalt asked us to meet him here?" Sally asked. "He sounded strange over the phone. I mean, he could have walked into our laboratory and asked to see us. I just don't get it."

Before Will could attempt to answer, another foghorn sounded in the distance. Water slapped against the barnacle-encrusted pilings of the dock. The smell of fish and the ocean filled the stagnant air.

"Damp out tonight," Will said, pulling his collar up to his chin. "Very damp."

As they made their way to the edge of the dock, a figure appeared, its long shadow falling on the rotted planks of the wharf.

"Dr. Cobalt, is that you?" Sally asked nervously.

The figure did not answer. It came closer. Finally, it stopped underneath the faint glow of a streetlamp.

"Dr. Cobalt, you startled us," Sally said.

"I'm sorry," Cobalt finally said. He was clad in a black raincoat and a wide-brim fedora, just like the ones people wore in black-and-white gangster movies. "I didn't mean to frighten you. Did you bring it? Did you bring what I asked for?"

Will spoke in his usual laid-back style: "Dr. Cobalt, dude, I realize you are our boss and everything, but meeting here in the middle of the night in this section of town is warped, don't you think? I'm cool with it and all, but couldn't this wait until morning when we're in our laboratory?"

"Yes, I agree, this is strange," Cobalt said, "but these are strange times, so I must ask you to give me the information I requested. It's imperative that I have it."

A damp breeze blew across the water, chilling Sally to the bone. She didn't like the idea of giving Cobalt her research, especially since it wasn't complete. She clutched the briefcase she was holding tighter. "I'm sorry, Dr. Cobalt," she said. "But this doesn't seem right to us."

"I suppose it doesn't," Dr. Cobalt said, "but

Mr. Grant and I need to see your discoveries no matter how incomplete they are."

Will smelled a rat and it wasn't the one he heard running along the dock. "My man, why don't you wait until we're finished, and we'll let you see everything. It'll be so sweet. I promise you that."

At that very second, Cobalt tipped the brim of his hat and two of Grant's goons stepped out from the shadows. One grabbed Sally and the briefcase. The other grabbed Will.

"I'm sorry, Sally. I'm sorry, Will," Cobalt said. "I'm sorry it has to end like this. I really like the two of you. I truly, truly do. Your research is groundbreaking. It's ingenious. But we need to use it for a higher purpose."

"Dude," Will said, "what's going on? Have you lost your mind?"

"Perhaps," Cobalt said. "But that's neither here nor there."

Still, Cobalt thought Will and Sally deserved
an explanation. He told them the foul story of
the Age Bug.

"How can you?" Sally yelled. "We put our hearts into this project. We could feed millions of people. Surely, someone as smart as you can see that. Now you want to harm people instead of helping them? You're a ghoul!"

"You will get no argument from me," Cobalt said softly. "I am a ghoul. It is out of my hands. These two gentlemen are going to take you on their boat for a ride out in the bay. I suspect we'll never see each other again, and I do regret that, I most certainly do. I want to thank you for your friendship. I enjoyed your company. And the pizza."

Cobalt then took charge of the briefcase and walked into the darkness.

Chapter 2

Checkmate

"Shh . . . she's concentrating."

Athena put her index finger to her mouth and shushed Tank before he could say something that probably wouldn't be very funny, and probably would be a bit ridiculous.

Tank took the hint and groaned. "I'm bored and I'm hungry," he grumbled. "Don't they serve hot dogs around here?"

"Listen, Tank," Gadget shot back in a hushed voice. "We come to your ball games to cheer you on. Now stop complaining and watch Pi. She's about ready to give Merriam B. Finkelbum a taste of his own medicine."

Pi looked her opponent square in the eye. Merriam saw the chessboard in front of him and took a deep breath. *There must be a way out,* he thought. *There just has to be. I can't believe this is happening to me. I'm Merriam B. Finkelbum. I'm the best chess player in the school district!*

Merriam felt like crying, but instead he doubled his efforts to find a solution. There wasn't one. The slight smirk on Pi's face told the whole story. Merriam's king was trapped like a fly in a spider's web. No matter where Merriam moved, danger awaited him.

Merriam pushed his thick-rimmed black glasses up his freckle-specked nose and let out a deep "I just wanna go home" sigh. He moved his king up one space, knowing it was fruitless. Pi moved her knight accordingly. Merriam's reign as the All-District Chess Champion was about to come crashing down on his red head.

"Check," Pi said.

Merriam did the only thing he could do. He moved his king one space to the left. Pi moved her queen in for the kill.

"Check," she said again.

Pi had lost to Merriam last year. Everybody lost to Merriam. But the three-time All-District Chess Champion had met his match. He knocked over his king, threw in the towel as they say, took off his glasses, and rubbed his weary eyes. The match was over. Pi was now the new All-District Chess Champion.

"Way to go, Pi!" Gadget yelled, clapping with the rest of the crowd.

"You go, girl," Athena cheered.

"Whoop . . . whoop . . . whoop," Tank yelled, pumping his fist high and fast into the air.

Pi smiled widely, pushing her long, black hair away from her flushed face. She shook Merriam's hand—it was clammy—and smiled. Pi's mom and dad jogged down from the stands and hugged and kissed their daughter. After the judges awarded Pi the All-District trophy, and after everyone snapped their cell phone photos, it was on to the Shake & Stir for some celebratory sodas and all the food anyone could eat, courtesy of Pi's parents.

¤

The Shake & Stir never had looked so good. Its white-and-red Formica tables gleamed in the glow of the fluorescent light. The restaurant was crowded, but the owner Doc himself came out and took their order.

"You were really great," Athena said, nibbling on her veggie burger. "I mean, Merriam didn't know what hit him. He's been champion for what, three years in a row? Even the high school kids can't beat him. Pi, you were like really, really amazing. The Gossip Gals are going to talk about you like crazy in the cafeteria on Monday! Where did you learn how to play chess like that?"

"My dad taught me," Pi said, smiling at her dad, who sat with her mom at a nearby table. "My mind works just like his, very mathematical, very logical. I fell in love with the game when I was seven and my dad won by a landslide. I've been trying to beat him ever since!"

"I think chess is boring," Tank said, munching on what was left of his double-bacon cheeseburger.

"Oh, Tank, you think any game you can't play with a ball or a puck is boring," Gadget said. "I mean, have you ever watched a baseball game? There's only fourteen minutes of action in a three-hour game."

"Get out, really?" Pi said.

"You lie, Gad old buddy," Tank said. "There's all sorts of action in a baseball game."

"I don't make this stuff up," Gadget replied. "The *Wall Street Journal* did a study about it. They also studied how much action there is in a pro football game. The average amount of time the ball is in play is eleven minutes."

"What sixth-grader reads the *Wall Street Journal*?" Tank shot back. "All I know is I love football, baseball, hockey, basketball, and soccer. Chess is as dry as Athena's veggie burger."

"You're such a dork burger," Athena said.

"But I love my cheeseburger," Tank said taking a big bite. "Where we goin' next?"

"I have to finish some homework before Monday," Gadget said, "so I'm off to the library once I finish my fries."

"I have to get home, too," Athena said. "D-Day gets mighty mad if I don't give him his cat food on time."

"I'm going to go home and relax," Pi said. "I've been practicing for this tournament all month and I have a test on Monday. Mom and Dad will drive you guys home."

That's exactly what Pi's parents did. First, they dropped off Tank, then Gadget, and finally Athena.

It was a wonderful day, or so it seemed.

Chapter 3

Empty House

Breckenridge Street in Webster's Corners was like most streets in this small town. Maple and oak trees lined the sidewalk. Mrs. Jenkins was sitting on her porch, across from Athena's house, as she always did no matter what the weather was like.

Mrs. Jenkins was the neighborhood gossip. Every neighborhood has one, the gossip, the blabbermouth, the nosy-Rosie-busybody who knows everything about everyone. Athena's mom called her the neighborhood watchdog. Athena's dad was less appreciative.

"She knows when we get up in the morning and when we go to sleep at night," Athena's dad once said. "Tell her a secret and within minutes the entire block knows. She's faster than the Internet."

"Oh, stop," Athena's mom would say. "She's just a lonely eighty-five-year-old woman. Her sons don't come to visit her anymore and her daughter is such a, well, let's just say she's not a very nice person. She's lived on this block since long before we got here. It's all she has. We're all she has."

Athena tended to agree with her mom.

"Hello, Mrs. Jenkins," Athena said, waving as she walked toward her front door.

"Hello, sweetheart," Mrs. Jenkins responded, waving back. "I didn't know your parents were going to have company today. I've never seen those people before. One was rather short and bald. Ugly too. The other, well, he didn't look very nice to tell you the truth. He had a thick beard and walked with a limp."

Athena didn't know what, or whom,

Mrs. Jenkins was talking about, and really didn't care. As far as Athena knew, nobody was visiting today. Nana was having toe surgery. As for Uncle Tim, well, he never came to visit, not since he married Aunt Christina. *What a dork burger*, Athena thought.

"Hi, I'm home!" Athena shouted as she walked through the front door. "You should have seen Pi. She was awesome. She won the championship. Then we all went out to the Shake & Stir to celebrate."

Silence.

"Mom . . . ? Dad . . . ? Are you home?"

Again, silence.

Athena walked into the kitchen. No one was there. She walked into the living room. No one was there either. The house suddenly felt too quiet.

"Mom . . . Dad . . . is anyone home? D-Day, come here buddy."

D-Day was nowhere to be found, which was strange. He always welcomed Athena when she came home.

Athena looked around the house. Nothing. She looked out the back window thinking her mom might be working in the flower garden or her dad might be trimming the hedges. Not a soul, even though both cars sat in the driveway.

By now Athena was worried. "Mom . . . Dad . . . are you home? Where are you?"

Athena ran upstairs into their bedroom.

Empty.

She bolted into the study.

What a mess!

Her parents' study was usually cluttered. There were too many early American and ancient Egyptian artifacts for Athena's taste, but that was to be expected. Her parents were archaeologists. Usually, the relics were carefully placed on the dozen or so shelves that lined the walls. Today, it looked like a tornado had blown through.

Everything was on the floor. The file cabinets and desk drawers were wide open and papers

had been strewn about. Chairs were knocked over. Lamps were broken.

Athena started to panic. "Mom . . . Dad . . . come out . . . Mom . . . Dad . . . where are you? Stop playing games!"

Then Athena heard a muffled cry coming from her bedroom. She ran up the stairs and into the room. Hearing another cry, she ripped open the closet door. Out jumped D-Day, looking frazzled.

"D-Day, oh my goodness, what happened? Where are Mom and Dad?"

D-Day let out a loud, sorrowful meow and ran into the study.

"Where are you going? Do you know what happened?"

D-Day most certainly did know what had happened. He had seen it all with his bright green eyes. He had seen the two strange men walk into the house and force Athena's parents into the study.

D-Day saw the men ransack the place, pulling out drawers and tipping over file cabinets. He saw them tie Athena's parents to their favorite chairs.

D-Day then saw one man, a particularly odd-looking bald man with a scar running down his cheek, hold a device up to Athena's parents' eyes. He pressed a button. The device emitted a red glow. The man muttered some words and then untied them.

D-Day then watched as Athena's dad went to the wall safe hidden underneath a map of the world, turned the combination lock, and removed several file folders.

That's when the other man—the one with the limp—kicked D-Day away. The cat scurried into Athena's room, the place he always felt safest. He opened the closet door with the tips of his tiny claws and crawled in beside Athena's old stuffed animals and a box of winter sweaters.

"D-Day, what happened? You need to tell me."

D-Day couldn't talk, but he did the next best thing. He ran underneath the desk in the study and returned with a well-worn and yellowed business card in his mouth.

"What's this?" Athena asked, pulling the card from D-Day's teeth. She looked at the card and read it. "What's Omni-Tech . . . ? And who are Sally and Will Snickerbloom?"

Chapter 4
Bragg Spills the Beans

Athena walked into her bedroom and picked up the access pad to the Amulator—the most powerful device in the world. She strapped the access pad to her wrist and pressed the panic app. If anyone would know what to do, it would be the Kid Squad. After all, they had saved the world from several catastrophes together. Within moments, she, D-Day, and the rest of the Kid Squad—Pi, Tank, and Gadget—magically materialized at Kid Squad headquarters.

"I came home from school and my parents were gone! I'm . . . I'm so scared," Athena cried, tears running down her rosy cheeks. She was holding D-Day tightly. "I mean, who . . . who were these men and what do they want with my parents? They're . . . they're . . . they're just boring archaeologists. I don't understand it one bit."

Pi put her arm around Athena's shoulders, trying to console her friend as best as she could. "I don't know either, but we'll find out, I promise," Pi said. "We'll find where your parents are and rescue them."

Just then the holophone buzzed, its eerie yellow-green light draping the Kid Squad headquarters in a somber glow. Dr. Ignatius Newton Stein and Colonel Ulysses T. Bragg, Director, US Army Special Projects, appeared.

They were thousands of miles away—Dr. I.N. Stein at his laboratory in the Amazon rain forest, Colonel Bragg at his secret lair—yet the holophone allowed both men to appear as if they were actually walking around Kid Squad headquarters, a series of chambers located under the basement of Pi's house.

"I see that we have an emergency," Dr. Stein began. "I was sitting down to, how do you say, ah yes, *brunch*. I was sitting down to zee brunch—a nice plate of poached eggs and cod, when zee panic alarm went off. Athena, zee dear girl, tell Colonel Bragg and myself what happened."

Athena sobbed as she told them the harrowing story of coming home and finding her house empty and her parents gone. She told them about how the wall safe was open and about the strange business card D-Day found.

"Oh, Dr. Stein, what happened to my mom and dad?" Athena cried as Pi again put her arm around her. "What happened to them?"

"Young lady, this is Colonel Bragg. Buck up. I order it. You gotta be tough. Because when the going gets tough, the tough get going."

Tank rolled his eyes.

Gadget looked embarrassed.

Athena cried harder.

Colonel Bragg rethought his approach. "Athena," he said in a voice that bordered on sweet, or as sweet as he could be. "I know this must be hard for you, but I promise we'll find your parents."

Then Colonel Bragg said something that shook everyone.

"I think I know what happened. And I think I know who has your parents."

The Kid Squad headquarters went silent. Gadget looked at Tank, who looked at Athena, who looked at Pi. Everyone was puzzled.

"You know *what*?" Tank asked.

"You know what happened to my mom and dad?" Athena repeated. "You know where they are? Let's go get them!"

Bragg hesitated for a second. He looked at Dr. Stein, who nodded in agreement. It was time to come clean.

"In due time, young lady," Colonel Bragg said. "They're not in any danger—yet."

Colonel Bragg then ran his fingers through his hair. He cleared his throat, sending an earsplitting echo over the holophone.

"First, I have something to tell you. Back in the 1980s, Will and Sally Snickerbloom were two of this country's most amazing scientists. They worked for a company called Omni-Tech. At the time, Omni-Tech was the world's leading scientific research company. They secretly developed many devices that the army still uses today. Under the direction of Dr. Stein, they even helped put together the Amulator."

Bragg then related the entire story of how Will and Sally thought they were manipulating genes for a new strain of wheat, when in reality they were working to develop the Age Bug.

"For this crazy colonel named Tecumseh S. Barnstable?" Gadget asked.

"Um, yes, and no," Bragg said. "You see, Barnstable was acting under special orders from the president of the United States. It was a top, top secret government project. Only those who needed to know about the Age Bug knew about the Age Bug. Not even Grant knew Uncle Sam was behind the project."

"We had to come up with, how you say, a *fib*," Dr. Stein said.

"You were part of this?" Pi asked.

"I was zee special adviser to zee president at zee time. It was my job to tell zee president zee progress of zee program."

"What was this, how do you say, little fib?" Tank asked, mimicking Dr. Stein's thick German accent.

"We had to come up with a cover story in case someone found out about the bug," Colonel Bragg said. "If anyone asked, Barnstable was a loony tune, a cracked egg. If it hit the papers or some nosy congressman or senator started asking questions, we set up Barnstable to take the blame."

"What was your role in all this?" Pi asked Colonel Bragg.

"I worked for Colonel Barnstable at the time, or more accurately, for the president. I was a young lieutenant. It was my job to keep an eye on things."

"How are my parents involved?" Athena asked, the tears now dried on her face.

"I'm getting to that, young lady," Bragg answered. "Somewhere along the line, things went horribly wrong. The owner of Omni-Tech was Oxford Grant. Grant was not the most noble person in this beautiful green world of ours. No, sir, he wasn't. He saw potential in the Age Bug and shopped it around to a few of our enemies . . . "

"Zee Russians were interested in zee bug," Dr. Stein said.

"That's right," Colonel Bragg shot back. "Those sneaky Russian spies couldn't wait to get their dirty mitts on the Age Bug. They paid Grant a whole lot of money to turn traitor. Back then, the Russians were our worst enemies. During the Cold War we had a lot of differences. They beat us to space; we beat them to the moon. Holy rocket launcher, I was determined that they weren't going to beat us at developing the Age Bug."

"I'm sorry, Colonel Bragg," Tank said. "I appreciate the history lesson and the walk down memory lane, but what in the wide world of sports does this have to do with Athena's mom and dad?"

Bragg was more than annoyed. "Stand down, Tank. I'm in charge here."

Tank's face reddened.

Bragg continued: "Anyway, working for Omni-Tech at the time was Dr. Alowishus

Cobalt, the man who more recently almost destroyed Earth with his Comet of Doom. Grant asked Cobalt to get the remaining research from the Snickerblooms and to, well, do away with them. Cobalt was young, but he wasn't stupid. He found out about Grant's decision to sell the Age Bug to the Russians. He also knew the value of Will and Sally's research. He double-crossed Grant and stole their work."

"What happened to the Snickerblooms?" Pi asked.

"Grant's henchmen kidnapped them as Grant had ordered and put them on a boat in San Francisco Bay. Just when the goons were about to toss Will and Sally overboard, yours truly, *Lieutenant* Ulysses T. Bragg, saved the couple from a watery grave.

"Barnstable and I had an inkling that Grant would turn traitor, but holy rocket launcher, Cobalt turning on Grant came right out of left field. We followed Cobalt to the dock that night and saw everything that happened. In the meantime, Cobalt got away . . . "

Tank snickered. "He does have a habit of doing that to you, doesn't he?" Tank teased. "Didn't you let him escape when we saved the world from the comet?"

Bragg ignored Tank and continued. "Cobalt got the Snickerblooms' research, except one very important formula that they held back. We didn't think much of it, because, dog-blasted, Cobalt believed Sally and Will Snickerbloom were gone forever. For the most part, they were.

"After I rescued them, they went to work for Uncle Sam, the good old US of A, on top secret projects. We gave them new identities. We changed their names, backgrounds, and professions. Heck, we even changed their fingerprints. That wasn't easy to do . . . "

Athena, by now, was annoyed. "What does this all have to do with my parents?" she asked in a stern voice.

Bragg looked at Dr. Stein. Dr. Stein looked at Bragg. There was a long pause between the two. The good doctor nodded once again.

"Will and Sally Snickerbloom are your parents, Athena," Bragg said.

The room went silent for the second time.

"You're lying, colonel," Athena shot back.

"There's no way that my parents are some government weapon makers who worked on who knows what for your stupid army. They're archaeologists, boring archaeologists who dig up mummies for a living."

"Dog-blasted, I'm telling the truth," Bragg said. "We gave them a new life so they, and later you, could be safe. Cobalt's the maddest scientist in the world. He'll do anything to get the Age Bug working. He and one of his close associates walked into your house this afternoon and kidnapped them."

"How do you know that?" Tank asked.

Bragg hesitated. Today was the day he was spilling all the beans. "Holy rocket launcher," Bragg said. "I'll just tell you everything. Athena's neighbor, Mrs. Jenkins, works for me. She keeps an eye on Athena and her parents. In fact, dog-blasted, I have a whole group of people that keep a watch on every one of you. I can't just

44

have one of our enemies come in and snatch you—and the Amulator access pads—right from under my nose. How would that look down at the Officers' Club?

"By the time Mrs. Jenkins alerted us—she's not as quick as she used to be—Cobalt, Athena's parents, and the missing formula were gone."

Athena sat on a chair, holding D-Day in her arms, trying to understand everything Colonel Bragg had just said. She stared blankly at the floor, not quite wrapping her head around the story. Her parents, it seemed, had been living a lie for years. They had lied to her, they had lied to Nana . . . was Nana even *Nana* or just one of Bragg's flunkies? Athena wasn't sure. She didn't know anything or anyone anymore.

"We have to find Cobalt before he develops the Age Bug," Bragg barked. "When he does—

and dog-blasted he will—no one is safe. Not you, not me, not your parents. Not the world. Who knows how he would use the weapon."

"Surely," Gadget interrupted, "the Snickerblooms, um, Athena's parents, won't work for him."

Dr. Stein answered Gadget. "In zee perfect world, *nein*, no, they would not work for zee evildoer. But Cobalt has zee ways of making people do what they do not want to do."

"How did Cobalt track down Athena's parents after all those years?" Pi asked.

"Well, young lady, it's a bit embarrassing," Bragg said. "It seems Cobalt had a spy in my command, a new recruit who pulled the wool over everyone's eyes. She told him many of our secrets."

It was all too much for Athena. She ran out the door into the night, not knowing who her parents were, or who she was.

"Should we go after her? I mean, her house has been ransacked . . . ," said Tank.

"Don't worry, I've got my people on this," Bragg said.

Chapter 5
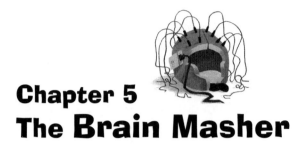
The Brain Masher

"You're mad, Dr. Cobalt, as mad as they come. Where are we, and what do you want from us?"

Athena's mother did not know what else to say. She and her husband, the former Will Snickerbloom, were in a bind, or as Athena liked to say, a pickle. Yes, they were in a major pickle.

Cobalt had shackled the pair to stainless steel chairs in a cold laboratory. The room was crammed with high-tech gadgets and science equipment. Armed sentinels stood guard near the exit, which could only be opened by a code entered on a keypad. More stood near a big steel door that led to who knew where. Sally looked for a way out. She didn't see any. Will stared at the ceiling, but all he saw were bright fluorescent lights.

Cobalt paced the laboratory, his hands rubbing his bald head, the heels of his pointy black shoes clicking against the cold, hard floor.

"Oh, Sally, you're such a drama queen. Always have been, always will be," Cobalt said. "Still, it is good to see you. It has been a while, hasn't it? I do miss those fun days at Omni-Tech."

"You weren't such a bad person back then," Sally offered. "You were a genius, smarter than anyone there. I even admired you. You could have made a really good scientist."

"What do you mean *could* have?" Cobalt said resentfully. "I *am* a good scientist . . . *great* even. A magazine even named me Evil Genius of the Year awhile back. It was in all the papers."

"We've followed your infamous career," Athena's father said. "I can't believe you are the same person that we used to know. What do you want from us? Where are we?"

"You're not in San Francisco anymore, Toto," Cobalt laughed. "I suppose you don't remember what we talked about when I was at your home kidnapping you?"

Silence.

"I didn't think so," Cobalt sighed. "That hypnosis ray I built, I call it the Hypno-ray, is as the kids say, a 'mean machine.' Do kids still say that? I don't think so.

"Anyway, I need to adjust it. It tends to erase a bit of short-term memory. As my granddad used to say, 'no harm, no foul.' It didn't seem to affect you too much."

Will and Sally waited for Cobalt to answer their questions. He cleared his throat and continued.

"Let me give you the scoop in twenty words or less. In short, you are here to finish your work on the Age Bug."

Cobalt's words rocked Will and Sally. For years they had tried and failed to forget about the Age Bug.

"When I took your work all those years ago, I quickly realized that you didn't give me all your research," Cobalt continued. "You left out one vital formula. I have it now. I found it in your wall safe."

Cobalt raised his left hand, which held a folder filled with papers. Athena's parents stared at the yellowed papers with amazement. They had tried to forget about their days at Omni-Tech too. It was so long ago, in a world that seemed distant and out of reach.

"Except the formula is still not complete," Cobalt barked, his voice bouncing off the laboratory walls. "That's because you have the remaining equations in your head, and I can't figure them out, no way, no how. You want to know why?"

"Is it because you're not the genius you think you are?" Sally said scornfully.

"Oh, no, that's not it, but nice try," Cobalt shot back. "It's that special code you used to write down your research. I've spent all these years trying to figure it out, but I couldn't. I had my top people working on it, too. The code stumped them. It's no wonder that toy soldier Bragg saved your life and put you to work for him. You were smart cookies. I do love cookies . . . chocolate chip especially . . . but that's neither here nor there, nor anywhere. I'm getting off track as I often do.

"All you have to do is decipher the code for me and add in the missing equations. Then I'll let you go home. I'll brew up a batch of the Age Bug and no one gets hurt. Easy as pie. Easy as A-B-C. As easy as 1-2-3."

"If we refuse?" Sally asked.

Cobalt sighed again. "Ah, yes. The ever-loyal Snickerblooms. Always trying to save humanity. Always trying to make life better for people. How *booooooooorrrrrrrrrrringggggggg*.

"Okay, let me spell it out for you. If you don't help me then I'll be forced to do something I *really, really, really, really* don't want to do. It's a grand experiment, perhaps my grandest. Okay, I know I always say every experiment is my grandest, even that whole Comet of Doom tractor beam thing a few months ago. This time I really mean it. In fact, it's behind Door Number Two."

Cobalt pointed to the big steel door where the guards were standing. "Johnny, if you please . . . "

On cue, the door opened and the man with the limp walked into the room. He and two of Cobalt's henchmen pushed a large cart containing various electronic devices. The whole setup looked like something out of an old Frankenstein movie, a chemistry experiment on steroids. Two more henchmen rolled in a pair of very human-looking robots. In fact, the robots looked a lot like Athena's parents.

Will and Sally gasped.

"A remarkable resemblance, don't you think?" Cobalt asked. "Here's what's going to happen if you don't do as I say."

Cobalt walked to Will and Sally holding a steel helmet outfitted with wires, electrodes, and lights. He placed the helmet on Will's head.

"If you don't do what I ask, I'm going to place this wonderful device that I call the Brain Masher on your heads. I will then plug the Brain Masher into that awesome-looking contraption that my colleagues just wheeled into the room. I will then put a similar device, although this one I call the Brain Builder, on my two Will and Sally bots.

"Once I finish that, I will walk over to that control table over there and push a button. When I push that button, everything that is inside your heads, all your knowledge, all your memories, all your dreams, will move through these wires and circuits and into my robots."

Will and Sally were stunned. They couldn't believe such a thing was possible. "Dude, you're a loony tune," Will said.

"Thank you, thank you very much," Cobalt said, impersonating Elvis, his favorite singer. "This whole weird science thing doesn't stop there, I'm afraid. My robots will have all your knowledge, including the ability to decode your research. They will finish your work on the Age Bug."

"And what happens to us?" Sally asked softly.

"That's a problem," Cobalt answered. "Not for me, but for you. I don't call it the Brain Masher for nothing. Unfortunately, once I activate the Brain Masher, you'll be left a vegetable and not one of those cute, talking cartoon vegetables you see on TV. You'll be like a rotten head of broccoli, a wilted stalk of celery, an overcooked carrot.

"You won't know who you are, where you are, or why you're there. You won't know which end is up, which end is down, or which end is an end. It will be as if you don't exist, only you do."

"You're mad," Sally said.

"You're a monster," Will said.

"Flattery will get you everywhere," Cobalt said, smirking evilly.

The room then went deathly quiet.

Cobalt walked back over to Sally and Will and took the Brain Masher off Will's head. He looked at the pair he had once called friends. A flood of memories came rushing back. *That was a different time, and I was a different Alowishus Cobalt*, he thought.

"So what shall you do, Mr. and Mrs. Snickerbloom?" he asked. "What shall you do?"

Chapter 6

Athena Meets a Friend

Athena ran as fast as she could all the way home. Darkness had descended on Webster's Corners and Athena smelled rain in the air as she passed Mr. Cambridge's house. She loved the roses that surrounded his iron fence. Athena's mom loved them, too. "They remind me of my grandma's garden," she'd say.

With all that had happened today, Athena wondered whether her mother had a grandma or any grandparents for that matter. Athena arrived home, bursting through the door with D-Day in tow. She ran straight to her room, jumped on her bed, and sobbed an ocean of tears as she hugged Froggie, her favorite childhood toy.

D-Day followed, walking across the bed, nuzzling his white face and pink nose against Athena's hands as she held Froggie close to her chest.

"Oh, D-Day, what am I going to do?" Athena cried. "We have to find Mom and Dad. Everyone thinks I'm an airhead, afraid of my own shadow. Let me tell you something right now, Colonel Bragg is a dorkus malorkus . . . a big fat liar. Mom and Dad are archaeologists. They are not government scientists!

"And that Mrs. Jenkins. The nerve. Where does she get off spying on me like that? Oh, D-Day, we're all alone. We have to find Mom and Dad, and once we do, we're going to quit the stupid Kid Squad and live a normal life. How does that sound?"

"Meoooooooooowwwwww," D-Day responded.

"I thought so," Athena said. "Where do we start?"

D-Day took the hint. Athena followed as the cat scurried into the dark study and disappeared in the shadows. Athena switched on the light and started to look around.

"What's in here, D-Day?" she asked.

Out of all the cats in the world, D-Day was the most amazing. If only he could talk. Athena knew that D-Day had special powers, a sixth sense. He was psychic, some would say. Athena just chalked up D-Day's abilities to being "one smart kitty." Still, for Athena, it didn't matter what made D-Day tick, as long as he did. She loved that cat to bitty-bit bits.

D-Day, true to form, walked over to the desk and rubbed up against the computer screen. Athena's dad never shut off the computer, and today was no different. The cat made sure his paw touched one of the keys on the keyboard, forcing the screen to come to life.

"What's on the computer, you big ball of fur?" Athena asked.

She clicked on her father's e-mail, which she would never do in a million years, and found a message addressed to her. *That's strange,* she thought. *I have my own e-mail account.*

Subject: Athena's Parents:

Athena, I know where your parents are. I want to help. Meet me in front of the Shake & Stir at nine o'clock tonight.
Your friend,
PDS

¤

By the time Athena reached the Shake & Stir, the rain was coming down in torrents. The wind had picked up, blowing leaves and plastic bags up and down the street. The restaurant had been closed for an hour. Athena's heart raced as she inched her way closer to the building.

"Good evening, Athena," a voice from the shadows announced. "So good of you to come."

The voice sounded foreign, but not foreign like Dr. Stein. The speaker, Athena thought, sounded like one of the characters on that snooze-fest of a TV show her parents watched on public television. Some show about the lives of rich people living in a big old house in England.

"Who are you and what do you want?" Athena asked as the rain soaked her clothes.

"May I introduce myself," the man said, refusing to come out of the shadows. "My name is Perceval D. Schmedly and I work for the notorious Dr. Cobalt."

Athena was about to run away when the man stepped into the light. He was wearing a black raincoat and carrying an umbrella. The rain ran off the umbrella like a waterfall. The man stood about six feet tall and walked with a limp. Athena could also see that Schmedly sported a thick dark beard. *That beard looks fake,* Athena thought.

"No reason to be afraid, my dear. Dreadful night, isn't it? I do apologize for the late hour.

I hope you don't mind. I'm terribly sorry. This weather makes my knee as stiff as a tree stump."

"What do you want?" Athena demanded.

"I want to help you. By helping you, you can help me," Schmedly said. "Your parents are safe, but I don't believe they'll be safe for long. Dr. Cobalt is a rather impatient fellow, you know. Rather a boor, too, but I won't bore you with the details."

Schmedly laughed at the pun. Athena did not.

Schmedly cleared his throat and continued. "I can help you and the rest of the Kid Squad free your parents."

"You know where my parents are?" she asked. "Tell me. Tell me where they are."

"In due time," Schmedly said.

Athena huffed. "What do you want in return?"

"Ah, good, right to the point. I like that," Schmedly said. "I want you to introduce me to Dr. Stein and Colonel Bragg. I have information they would like to know . . . important information. You see, I'm Dr. Cobalt's right-hand person, so to speak, although I am left handed."

Athena didn't laugh, and Schmedly looked embarrassed even under the umbrella. "Probably not a time for jokes, I dare say. I'm dreadfully sorry. To the point. I'm privy . . . you know what privy means, don't you?"

Athena nodded.

"Ah, a smart one too. Wonderful, simply wonderful. I'm privy to classified information about Dr. Cobalt and some of the more notorious types he hangs around with. You and the other members of the Kid Squad have battled them before. I believe Dr. Stein and Colonel Bragg would want to know what information I have to offer."

"Is that all you want? An introduction?"

"From you, yes. From them, no, of course not. I want to sell them what information I have. If they dismiss me and tell me to go on my way, well, a bargain is a bargain, and I shall help you free your parents."

Suddenly, across the street, a group of Cobalt's henchmen sprung from behind several parked cars. Their Freeze Rays were all aimed at Schmedly. "There he is!" one yelled. "There's the traitor."

Schmedly reached for his own Freeze Ray before someone shouted, "Don't try it, Percy ole chap. I'll freeze you like a Popsicle. Come with us and no one gets hurt. You too, miss."

Athena's eyes widened with terror. One of the men walked up to Schmedly. "Thought you could sell the boss out for a few bucks, didn't you, Percy. I told the boss not to trust you, but he never listens to me. Maybe now he will."

Cobalt's henchmen pushed Athena and Schmedly into a black SUV. As they pulled away, D-Day, looking like a wet rat, ran toward Kid Squad headquarters, flying through puddles. He had a lot to say. If only he could speak!

Chapter 7
An **Old Friend Returns**

Will looked at Sally. Sally looked at Will. "I guess we have no choice," Sally said to Cobalt. "We'll finish the Age Bug."

"Excellent," Cobalt said. "You'll get to work right away. Oh, joy. You won't be sorry. I am so, so happy, although I was looking forward to turning you into Will and Sally bots. Just joking. I'm a kidder."

Will and Sally weren't so sure. They slipped on the lab coats that Cobalt had given them and got down to business. Hours, perhaps days seemed to pass as Will and Sally toiled under what some would consider harsh conditions. Three armed guards stayed in the laboratory to make sure Will and Sally did their work.

Cobalt constantly walked in, looked over their shoulders, and then went away. They ate only peanut butter and banana sandwiches.

As Will and Sally were eating their lunch, a piercing alarm cut through the building, causing Will to drop his sandwich. Red lights flashed and voices barked over the loudspeaker. Guards ran to their battle stations. A blast outside rocked the building.

"Bragg!" Cobalt yelled, visibly upset. "That tin soldier found me. Blast! Blast! Blast!"

The mad scientist raced to his office and moved his desk from where it sat. Underneath the carpet was an escape hatch. It led to a secret tunnel and a space pod that would whisk Cobalt away to his hideout on Mars.

As he tried to pull the hatch door open—it was stuck—Cobalt could hear the battle outside.

In the laboratory, Will and Sally hid underneath a table and held each other tight.

Explosion after explosion rocked the room, tossing test tubes and beakers to the floor.

Blam! Kaboom!

When the smoke cleared, Will and Sally saw a gaping hole where the large steel door had once been.

Cobalt's guards readied for action. They aimed their Freeze Rays at the opening. The invaders marched in, aiming special rays of their own and used them with amazing accuracy. Their weapons cemented Cobalt's thugs to the floor.

Back in his office, Cobalt tried desperately to open the escape hatch. "Darn, darn, darn!" he shouted.

"Time to face the music," Cobalt said, mimicking a favorite cliché his mother always used. He grabbed a stun ray from his arsenal and marched out of his office. "I won't go down without a fight," he muttered to himself.

As he walked down the hall toward the laboratory, he noticed things were eerily silent. He steadied himself as he hit the numbers to the keypad lock.

"Come and get me, Bragg," Cobalt yelled defiantly as the door slid open. His finger was on the trigger, ready to freeze anyone who stood in his way.

The door opened. Cobalt expected to see Bragg, his troops, and those "pesky Kid Squad urchins." Instead someone else appeared. At first Cobalt did not know who it was.

"Good evening, Alowishus," the man said. "I hope you don't mind the unexpected visit. Your guards outside weren't very hospitable, but my bots, the best in the world, convinced them otherwise."

Oxford Grant stood towering above Cobalt. Sweat dripped from his round head, which he patted dry with a red handkerchief.

Cobalt tried to hide how astounded he was to see his old boss again. "Well, well, well, if it isn't my old friend and employer. To what do I owe this honor, you old has-been."

The robots aimed their stun guns on Cobalt's shiny noggin.

"Alowishus, my boy," Grant said. "Good to see you, too. Good to see you, indeed. I see you still like drama. I didn't think we'd ever see each other again, after the way you ran off when Bragg and Barnstable came to get me. You ran faster than a rabbit being chased by a hound."

"Get to the point," Cobalt said.

"While you were as free as a bird, I spent three decades in jail courtesy of Uncle Sam and Barnstable, that two-faced traitor. Now I'm out and madder than ever."

"Good for you," Cobalt interrupted. "When did they release you?"

"Ha! Release me?" Grant said, astounded. "I broke out of their puny prison about a month ago. I had a lot of time to think in there. For thirty years I've been planning my sweet, sweet revenge. What is it that Shakespeare said, 'revenge is a plate of cold cuts?'"

"'A dish best served cold,' you moron, not cold cuts," Cobalt shouted. "Why would you want to get revenge on me? I didn't do anything to you. All I did was escape before they slapped me in irons. I became a well-known evil scientist. Perhaps you've read about me."

"Oh, Alowishus," Grant said. "Believe it or not, the world doesn't revolve around you."

Cobalt looked shocked. *Really? The world doesn't revolve around me?* He shrugged.

"You're not the one I want revenge against. On the contrary, I have a proposition for you," Grant said. "Through the grapevine I heard that you, along with Will and Sally Snickerbeetle, Snickerdoodle, whatever their names are, are up to your old Age Bug tricks again. I want in."

Will and Sally emerged from under the table where they were hiding and looked at Grant with contempt.

"And why would I let you in?" Cobalt asked.

"For one thing, if you don't, my heavily armed bots will make frozen mincemeat out of you," Grant warned. "Second, if you and I finish the Age Bug—maybe keep a little for ourselves—we'll sell the rest, just like we were going to do all those years ago. We'll make billions this time. Billions!"

"Who's going to buy it?" Sally yelled. "The Russians? The Cold War is over, Grant."

"Oh, Sally, I can sell a coffin to a corpse," Grant said. "I happen to know the names of several evil people that would love to get their hate-filled hands on our little bug. What do you say, Alowishus old boy? Are you in or are you out?"

It was a toss-up as to what Cobalt loved more— money, power, or fame. In his screwed-up mind they all were one and the same, each a part of the other. With billions of dollars in his greedy little hands, Cobalt could rule the world, or at least a small corner of it. *Gosh darn, I want to rule the world but never got the chance,* Cobalt thought. *I might even get a reality show. How smack-down awesome would that be?*

Cobalt stared at Grant. Grant stared at Cobalt. The two maniacs shook hands. At precisely that moment, Cobalt's men brought Schmedly and Athena into the laboratory.

Athena spotted her parents and ran to them. All three embraced.

"Oh, Mom, oh, Dad, I thought I'd never see you again," Athena said. "Mr. Schmedly was going to help me rescue you, but Cobalt's goons came and got us."

"Good work, Schmedly," Cobalt said. "You got our little Kid Squad pipsqueak. Now there's no stopping her parents from making an Age Bug that actually works."

Athena was aghast. "You mean, you weren't going to help me rescue my parents?" she asked Schmedly.

"Oh, heavens no, young lady, why would I do such a thing?" Schmedly said in the most British of accents. "You see, Dr. Cobalt is a very smart evil man, my little fish and chips. He was afraid that your parents would snooker him and his little project. We needed insurance that your parents would work faithfully and on time. You're that insurance."

"That's right, little girl," Cobalt said. "Your parents have been yanking my chain. They've been making a new type of dishwasher detergent instead of my Age Bug."

Cobalt waved an accusing finger at Will and Sally. "A first year chemistry student could spot your trick a bazillion miles away. If you didn't know, there's no such thing as a bazillion, but you get the point. Now get to work, and don't try to pull the wool over my eyes. It makes me itch.

"Schmedly, my friend, would you be a good chap and hook up Athena to the Brain Masher?"

Will and Sally lunged to stop Schmedly, but two guards blocked them.

"Now, let's all get to work. Go, team, go!" Cobalt said, sounding like a high school cheerleader. "Give me an A! Give me a G! Give me an E! Give me a . . . ah, you know the rest. Age Bug! Age Bug! Rah! Rah! Rah!"

Chapter 8
Stop 'n' Save Chaos

Webster's Corners is a fine town with a small but fine grocery store. In fact, it's the only grocery store in town. There's no need for a second. Located on Main Street across from Pie in Your Eye Bakery, the shelves of the Stop 'n' Save brim with every type of food anyone could want.

Got a hankerin' for a box of oatmeal raisin cookies? The Stop 'n' Save has ten different kinds. Organic milk, check. Creamy whipped garlic butter, check. The candy aisle goes on forever. As for the snack aisle, let's not even go there. It's a coach potato's dream come true.

Not only does the Stop 'n' Save have it all, but it is also a popular meeting place where gossip can be heard in every aisle.

Who bought Fred's Gas & Guzzle on Louise Boulevard? Don't wait for the announcement in next week's *Citizen's News*. Sarah Smith, who works reception in Dr. Eisler's office, spilled the beans in Aisle 3, right near the toilet bowl cleaners.

Who's that new hairdresser at Tamara's Cut & Style? Just ask Becky Pondo in the frozen food section.

Ah, yes, the Stop 'n' Save has it all, including the black licorice that Gadget and Tank loved so much.

It was early in the morning, around eight o'clock, and the boys were on their way to school when they decided to drop by the store and pick up some licorice.

The whole situation with Athena's mom and dad had gnawed at them. But there was little Tank, Gadget, Pi, and Athena (wherever she was) could do. Bragg had kept his mouth shut about the whole episode since that day at Kid Squad headquarters.

"At ease," he had told the kids. "I know what I'm doing. Go to school and act normal. When I need you, I'll call for you."

So it went for three days going on four. Athena hadn't been at school, but they figured Bragg had the situation under control. As Gadget and Tank entered the grocery store, they saw Mr. McPherson, the store manager, putting bread on the shelf. Suzie Warman waited in line to check out. Pete Driscoll was at the next register buying donuts, milk, and spicy beef jerky. *The breakfast of champions*, Tank thought.

There were a few people in the meat aisle, and the deli crew was cleaning the slicers to a high shine. In Aisle 4, near the boxes of macaroni and cheese, a stranger stood.

Gadget and Tank had never seen the person before, but that wasn't surprising. They had to get their candy and roll off to school. Still, something was odd about the guy.

Gadget and Tank found what they were looking for and started walking over to a cash register. That's when the stranger appeared at the front of the store. He took a glass ball out of his pants pocket. Then he reached into his camouflage coat and pulled out something even more troubling.

"Is that a gas mask?" Gadget said. "Holy guacamole, Tank, it is."

Gadget instinctively reached for the access pad on his wrist. He pressed a couple of buttons and an invisible, airtight bubble engulfed him and Tank. The stranger put on the gas mask and then smashed the glass ball against the floor.

The ball shattered into a thousand pieces. Then the stranger did something truly bizarre. He pulled out a digital video camera and filmed something worthy of the best horror movie Hollywood could produce.

Suzie, who was no more than twenty, suddenly turned into a 110-year-old woman. Her skin wrinkled like a weathered piece of leather. Her bright blonde hair with its red and green streaks turned white. Her whole body seemed to slump with age.

Mr. McPherson, who was forty-five and had a mane of deep red hair, now looked like Tank's great-grandfather—old, bald, and short, with more hair coming out of his ears than Tank's dog had. The bread tray Mr. McPherson was carrying fell to the floor with a great crash. It was just too heavy for him.

The scene played out all across the Stop 'n' Save. The deli crew moaned in pain, their once young bones now brittle and weak. Jason, the bagger, had walked into the backroom a robust sixteen-year-old. He stumbled out looking as if he had lived for a century and a half.

The man with the video camera, deciding he had seen enough, casually strolled out of the grocery store and into a nearby van.

Gadget and Tank, protected by the Amulator's bubble, looked around in terror.

¤

"That dog-blasted Cobalt has the Age Bug," Colonel Bragg yelled over the holophone. "Athena's parents must have been working overtime. Where is that girl, anyway?"

"You know where she is as well as I do," Pi said. "Cobalt has her. She's in danger."

"*Unglaublich*, unbelievable," Dr. Stein said. "Zee Cobalt has perfected zee Age Bug. If we do not do something, we will all be *kaput*. All that madman has to do is put zee bug in zee water supply or drop a bomb on Main Street and we will all be, how do you say, *ancient*. Yes, we will all be ancient."

"Not quite, Dr. Stein," Colonel Bragg interrupted. "We have a little time. My best people descended on the Stop 'n' Save once Gadget and Tank alerted us. It seems the Age Bug wore off in about an hour. Will and Sally haven't perfected the formula yet, or they're just stalling. Everything, and everyone, is back to normal. We used the Forgetful Beam to erase the memory of the attack from the minds of those involved. It's like it didn't even happen."

"Holy guacamole," Gadget said, "It did happen and we were there. If it wasn't for the Amulator, Tank and I would have been 100 years late for school!"

"What in the wide world of sports are we gonna do?" Tank asked. "We need to do *something* and right now. We need to stop Cobalt and rescue Athena and her parents."

"Tank is right," Pi said. "We need to move fast, before the Age Bug turns us all into golden oldies."

"You're right," Bragg barked. "Holy rocket launcher, you're right. I've been waiting for the right moment, for Cobalt to let down his guard. It's time to move. I know where Cobalt is. Cobalt and Grant. Those two misfits joined forces and intend to sell the Age Bug. I'm sure they'll keep a little for themselves, too. Dog-blasted it's time for action.

"I should have buried Grant and Cobalt back in 1987. But orders are orders and the president told me to be nice. Just throw them in jail, the president said. I didn't even vote for the guy. I'm done being nice."

Tank laughed. "You mean you were nice once? I find that hard to believe."

"Here's what we're going to do," Bragg continued. "Make sure your access pads are juiced. Dog-blasted! We're going in."

Chapter 9
Battle at Salty Sarah's

"I don't care what the video shows," Grant yelled. "Your man left too early. The Age Bug didn't work. They turned old for an hour, and then everyone became young again. Cobalt, you fool, the Snickerbeetles, Snickerdoodles, whatever their names are, have pulled the proverbial wool over your eyes again."

Cobalt, as evil as he was, didn't know how to respond except to say "wool makes me itchy." The Age Bug worked, then it didn't work, and he was furious. He looked at Will and Sally, his piercing stare cutting a hole through them all the way to the other side of the laboratory. There, Athena lay bound to the Brain Masher.

"What do you have to say for yourselves?" Cobalt asked in a voice as cold as a winter storm. "You don't want Athena's brain to be turned into sauerkraut, do you? I hate sauerkraut, but I do love kielbasa. Explain yourselves! Why did this happen?"

Will and Sally looked at each other and shrugged.

"Something went wrong, Dr. Cobalt," Sally said matter-of-factly.

"You think?" Cobalt shot back sarcastically. "Is that all you can say? 'Something went wrong, Cobalt?' I know something went wrong, but what?"

"We manipulated the genes of the bacterium as they should have been manipulated," Will said. "Theoretically, everyone should have stayed old, but they didn't."

"Unless . . . ," Sally interrupted.

"Unless what, my sweet Mrs. Snickerbloom,

although I know that's not your last name any longer?" Cobalt said.

"Unless we approached the science from the wrong direction," Sally said thoughtfully. "We were able to turn the age gene on, but then it chemically overrode itself and turned off, sort of like a light on a timer."

"So what?" Grant barked.

"What we actually did, in a manner of speaking, is stop the aging process. The gene made the people as old as it could, then *poof!* The process reversed itself. With a little more manipulation, we can find out why and then be able to turn the age gene off for good."

Cobalt looked at Sally quizzically. He nodded in agreement. "You discovered how to stop the aging process," he said to no one in particular. "Interesting. Very interesting."

Will thought quickly. "Dude, there's more money to be made in developing antiaging technology than in developing something that makes people old," he said. "Heck, people spend billions of dollars every year on creams and all sorts of other rubbish to keep young. Now they don't have to work so hard. When people get to the age they want to be, we can turn off the age gene and they won't get any older. Think of the implications. We can probably make a pill they can take."

Cobalt put his finger to his chin and said, "Interesting," again to no one in particular. His mind quickly went through all the various scenarios. Yes, he could make billions of dollars marketing the antiaging technology to billions of people. Yes, they would line up for miles to get the pill. Yes, he could charge them whatever amount of money he wanted. He could be swimming in cash in no time.

In the end, though, for an evil scientist of Cobalt's caliber, evil has a way of clouding a person's thinking. He thought of something that would put him in the Evil Scientist Hall of Fame, if there were such a thing.

"Hear me out," Cobalt finally said. "If you can turn the age gene off, it should be rather simple to reverse it. Kind of like hitting the rewind button on one of those old VCRs. Do kids still use VCRs? I don't think so."

Grant quickly looked up, raising his thick, bushy eyebrows. He understood exactly what Cobalt was saying and he wasn't mad anymore. He was almost giddy.

"You might have something there, Alowishus, my boy," he grumbled, his face moist with sweat. "Instead of turning people into grandmas and grandpas, we can turn them into tiny tots, little drooling children that puke on everybody. We can explode the Age Bug over an army and in seconds, the troops will be whiny little brats, crying for their mommies or their commanding officers. Can it be done?"

Grant shot Will and Sally a glance, as did Cobalt. Sally spoke first, and softly. "I suppose so."

"Wonderful," Cobalt broke in. "Simply wonderful. What a team we have here. Just like the old days. What a group. Let's go, team, go!" Cobalt was in cheerleader mode again.

"If we refuse?" Will said.

Cobalt nodded toward Athena. Schmedly turned the screws tighter on the Brain Masher.

¤

Back in the day, Webster's Corners was the pretzel capital of the world, or so the town liked to brag. There were five, count 'em, *five* pretzel factories located in the south end of town.

If you walked through the neighborhood on any given day, you could smell the fresh aroma of baking pretzels wafting through the air. Salty Sarah's Pretzels was the queen of the five cracker companies, but Salty Sarah's had gone out of business years ago.

Yet, the redbrick factory with a huge billboard of Salty Sarah herself—she wore a white sailor's cap and held a huge pretzel—was still there, vacant, or so most people thought. Two smokestacks towered over the building, and ivy crawled up the wall facing the setting sun. A few of the windows had been shattered by bored teens, and the steel doors that led into the building had been rusted shut for years.

Colonel Bragg, Dr. Stein, Gadget, Tank, Pi, and Bragg's small company of troops hid in the bushes of the overgrown parking lot across the street. A broken chain link fence circled the lot. Its asphalt was cracked. Unwanted plants grew from the crevices. Bragg trained his binoculars on the building.

"Cobalt's laboratory is inside that building," Bragg whispered. "When my team storms the building, you kids will use the Amulator and make yourselves invisible. Find Athena, free her, and whisk her out as soon as you can. Dog-blasted, it's too bad she doesn't have her access pad. If I've told you kids once, I've told you a million times, don't leave home without it.

"Once you get her out of harm's way, my team and I will do the rest. She's on the third floor of the factory all the way in the back. Be careful, she's hooked up to some brain scrambling device. If you can, destroy the device before you free her, without destroying her."

"How do you know this?" Gadget asked.

"Let's just say I do," Bragg answered.

"Kids, be very careful," Dr. Stein warned. "Zee Age Bug is a very dangerous weapon. Cobalt must have figured out what is wrong with zee bug by now. If you inhale zee bug this time, it will not reverse itself. Keep your masks on!"

Pi, Tank, and Gadget were worried. They all thought the same thing: *I'm too young to be old.*

"Let's move," Bragg said.

With that order, the Kid Squad sprang into action. They turned themselves invisible and ran to the front of the Salty Sarah's factory. Bragg's team moved on the building from all sides as black helicopters swooped in from the north.

Bragg's team was the best of the best. The highly-trained troops stormed the front and side doors of the old factory, while an armored vehicle pummeled the entrance to the loading dock in back.

Men and women in black uniforms and dark glasses, all wearing gas masks, climbed ropes up to the top floors as if they were scaling a mountain. Others dropped down from ropes suspended from the helicopters. They busted the windows with steel boots and tossed sleeping gas canisters down hallways and into rooms.

Pi, Tank, and Gadget could hear the alarms go off inside the building as they walked through the front door and up the stairs to where Athena and her parents were.

¤

"This time it's Bragg and those Kid Squad brats for sure," Cobalt moaned. "But I'm ready for them. They're probably invisible. They are so predictable. They should turn themselves into ants, or robins. Always invisible."

"Don't worry, Alowishus, my bots can handle anything that Bragg's soldiers can dish out," Grant said.

Cobalt's guards put up a tough fight, as did Grant's bots. All used their Freeze Rays and iced down many of their opponents. Explosion after explosion rocked the old pretzel factory as the sleeping gas continued to creep through the building. Old bags of flour, which had sat in the corner on the third floor for years, ripped open, turning everyone shades of white.

Pi, Gadget, and Tank, still invisible, walked into the laboratory and saw Athena strapped to the table. Cobalt, figuring the Kid Squad was around, turned on a special ultraviolent light that made Pi, Gadget, and Tank visible.

"Alert!" one of Grant's bots shouted in a mechanical voice. "Alert! Stop them from freeing the girl."

The robots aimed their Freeze Rays on the Kid Squad, but Gadget was faster. He hit a few buttons on his access pad and shielded his friends with a special force field.

"Take that, you buckets of bolts," Tank shouted.

It was too soon to get confident, though.

Some of Cobalt's men snuck up on the trio from behind, each grabbing a member of the Kid Squad. Sally and Will felt like they were in an action movie. And they couldn't figure out why Athena's friends were battling the robots. *What are those devices on their wrists?* Sally wondered.

"What in the world are Athena's friends doing here?" shouted Will. "Wait until their parents find out."

Of course, Sally had no idea her daughter and the others were members of the ultra-secret Kid Squad. As the guards began dragging Pi, Tank, and Gadget away from Athena, another familiar figure appeared in the doorway.

D-Day was always itching for a good fight, and he didn't want to be left out of this one, especially since Athena was in danger. He had followed everyone to Salty Sarah's Pretzel Factory.

Like a lion leaping for its prey, D-Day flew through the air onto the shoulders of the guard who was dragging Gadget. The cat bit the man's ear.

"Ouch," the guard yelled, releasing Gadget and grabbing his earlobe. Gadget turned around quickly and used the Amulator's cement ray to turn the guards dragging Pi and Tank to stone.

As the fighting raged, Grant silently slid over to Will and Sally's workstation and grabbed a flask filled with the Age Bug. He put on a gas mask that was sitting on the table and held the tube in his hand. Dr. Stein had finally made it to the laboratory. He saw Grant and pounced, trying to grab hold of the flask, but a robot knocked Dr. Stein to the ground.

"Holy guacamole," Gadget said. "I've seen this show before."

Grant smashed the flask onto the hard floor. Suddenly, everyone in the room, except the bots, turned into toddlers. The Age Bug worked . . . but in reverse, just as Cobalt had hoped. Dr. Stein, now two years old, looked comical in his long, flowing lab coat. His hair still had its fright-wig look, but now it sat on a child's head.

Cobalt's goons turned into crying children, their uniforms wrapped around them like baby blankets. Will and Sally were children, too. Will was laughing as he grabbed Sally's hair. Cobalt's laboratory looked like a day care.

Luckily, D-Day, Athena, Pi, Tank, and Gadget were safe. Gadget had activated the Amulator just in time and created that oh-so-airtight bubble.

Grant, his gas mask making him look especially sinister, walked over toward Athena and flipped on the switch to the Brain Masher. She was in the bubble, but the switch was not!

"Foil me, you little brats? I think not," Grant shouted. "I will get my revenge, even if it is on this one child."

The Brain Masher started to come to life.
Grant looked on with glee. Gadget, Pi, and Tank
were helpless. If Gadget lifted the protective
shield, they would all inhale the Age Bug. And
they couldn't get the machine off her head!

Grant laughed maniacally as the Brain Masher started to do its dirty work. Across the room, Schmedly appeared, donning his own gas mask. "What do you think you're doing?" Schmedly asked, his British accent suspiciously absent.

Schmedly held up a Freeze Ray of his own. He aimed it at Grant and pulled the trigger. The ray knocked Grant for a loop. Schmedly then rushed off and shut down the Brain Masher before it could harm Athena.

With Grant incapacitated, more of Bragg's troops tumbled into the laboratory. They short-circuited Grant's robots with a series of e-bombs that fried the robots' electronic brains.

The fighting was over, but the crying wasn't. All of the troops, good and evil, were bawling their eyes out, although Will was still busy pulling Sally's hair. Some were tired, others hungry. Dr. Stein cried for his mom.

Bragg brought in two industrial-sized fans to blow all the contaminated air out of the laboratory. What was left of the Age Bug harmlessly dissipated into the atmosphere.

"It's okay, gang," Bragg said. "You can turn off the protective shield."

Gadget did as he was told. He, Pi, and Tank went straight to work to free Athena from the Brain Masher.

Bragg then walked over to Schmedly, who had handcuffed Grant to a metal table. Bragg shook Schmedly's hand.

"Good to see you again," Bragg said.

"It's good to see you, too," Schmedly said. He then took off the gas mask and fake beard. Schmedly wasn't Schmedly any longer. He was Colonel Barnstable, Bragg's old boss.

"I'm glad I convinced you to come out of retirement," Bragg said. "You did a heck of a job. Thanks for all the information and for keeping an eye on everything."

"Thank you, Colonel," Barnstable said. "It felt good to be useful again. You're never too old to make a difference. The Age Bug will wear off in about an hour, I made sure of that. Everybody will be normal again—even Dr. Stein over here."

The toddler Dr. Stein was playing with Will and Sally, tugging on their lab coats.

"We should round up Cobalt's goons and put them in a playpen before they grow up," Barnstable said. "Where is that bald-headed coward, anyway?"

While the fighting was raging, Cobalt had finally got the escape hatch in his office open. He had squeezed his evil body into the secret tunnel and escaped, as he always did.

"You know something, Colonel?" Barnstable said. "We shouldn't have developed the Age Bug to begin with. No one should play with people's lives like that."

"You're right, my old friend," Bragg said, his voice trailing off. "You're right."

Chapter 10

Shake & Stir Pizza

"Cheer up, Pi. You did your best," said Gadget. "It was a tough tournament. You were one move away from going to the state finals. No one from Copernicus Middle School ever made it to the finals of the county tournament before, not even Merriam B. Finkelbum. You were the first."

Gadget was right, but Pi shook her head in disbelief. "I don't understand why I didn't see that move. I just don't. It was so easy and it was staring me in the face. Ugh."

The All-County Chess Tournament had ended badly for Pi. She had made it to the finals, but a curly-haired kid from Emerson Middle School in Cornwall Hollow took her king.

"Zee chess is a very, how do you say, *funny* game. Yes, zee chess is a very funny game," Dr. Stein offered between bites of macaroni and chicken wing pizza, a specialty at the Shake & Stir. "I never, how you say, got zee hang of it."

The restaurant was busy as usual for a Saturday afternoon. The gang, along with Dr. Stein and Colonel Bragg, had made their way to the eatery after Pi lost the chess tournament.

Everyone seemed to be having a good time, except Athena.

She looked sad staring off into space.

"Hey, Athena," Tank said. "You should have a slice of pizza. Doc really picked a good one."

Athena didn't say a word.

"Hey 'thena, don't look so down," Pi said, trying to comfort her friend. "I'm the one who lost the tournament."

"I know, Pi," Athena said, twirling her strawberry blonde hair. "I'm just so mad at my parents for lying to me all these years. I had no idea who they really were. How am I supposed to trust them again?"

"Young lady, don't be too hard on your parents," Bragg said, sipping a soda. "I feel partly responsible, but holy rocket launcher, we all did what we had to do all those years ago."

"I suppose," Athena said softly. "Why didn't they tell me? Heck, I can keep a secret. I'm a member of the Kid Squad for goodness' sake. What's more secret than us?"

"I suspect your parents did not want to put you in zee danger, which they finally found themselves in," Dr. Stein said. "They wanted to keep you safe. They love you very much."

Athena thought about that and simply shrugged and sighed. In time, Athena would get over her parents' secret life. In time.

Everyone sat silently for a second before Tank spoke up. "Are you sure Athena's mom and dad won't remember anything that happened?" he asked. "Did you see their faces when we materialized at the factory? You could have knocked your mom down with a feather duster, Athena."

"The Forgetful Beam is one hundred percent effective. I'll bet dollars to donuts on that," Bragg said. "It'll erase their memory about everything that has happened. In fact, we programmed the device to wipe out all of their knowledge on the Age Bug."

Bragg smirked slightly, or as much a smirk as he could muster with that stone face of his. "What's funny is that the Forgetful Beam was actually invented for Barnstable and me by Sally and Will in the late '80s."

"Speaking of Barnstable," Gadget said, "he was a pretty good spy."

"You got that right, young man," Bragg said. "Barnstable has been part of Cobalt's crew for the past several months, letting me know what he's up to. The colonel is experienced and knows his way around a catastrophe or two. I've used him a few times in the past, but this was his biggest case."

"What happens to the Age Bug now?" Pi asked.

"Zee Age Bug is *kaput*," Dr. Stein said. "It is, how you say, too dangerous and should never have been developed. We destroyed all of the research."

"What about Cobalt?" Tank asked. "When do you expect to see him again?"

Everyone at the table went silent again as they thought about Cobalt and the mess he always made of things. Cobalt was like a piece of gum on the bottom of a shoe. No matter how hard you tried to get rid of it, there was always some left.

Everyone at the table knew they would see the evil Cobalt again. They hoped it wasn't too soon.